AuthorHouse™
1663 Liberty Drive
Bloomington, IN 47403
www.authorhouse.com
Phone: 1 (800) 839-8640

This book is printed on acid-free paper.

ISBN: 978-1-7283-3627-5 (sc)
ISBN: 978-1-7283-3628-2 (hc)
ISBN: 978-1-7283-3626-8 (e)

Print information available on the last page.

Published by AuthorHouse 11/15/2019

authorHOUSE®

To my parents
Aloysio & Maria da Penha

To my partner Philippe,

and our children
Corey & Kelly

LEONARDO
AND
THE BLACK & WHITE RAINBOW

Dr. Fabiano Rabelo DeMoraes

On one given morning Leonardo, a boy who lived in the Land of Black and White, woke up and felt his heart speaking of something he was yet to know: Colors.

But as he looked around, he realized everything was Black and White; there were no colors.

Suddenly that colorful moment in his heart disappeared, and his disappointment was reflected in his eyes.

Leonardo longed for his life also to be full of colors.

So he then made a decision; he was going to paint the rainbow!

He had heard that the rainbow should be full of colors! But the rainbow up in the sky, in the land where Leonardo used to live, had only two colors.

Since he could not find any colors in the Land of Black and White, Leonardo decided to travel and look for them somewhere else; in the Land of Colors.

The next morning, he started his journey to the colorful land.

When he finally arrived in the Land of Colors, he picked the most beautiful flowers, with the most incredible colors from the most spectacular gardens that ever existed!

The flowers turned into the most amazing colors for him to paint the Black and White rainbow:

Red, Yellow, Pink, Green, Blue, Orange and many other colors and shades.

Leonardo dreamed of making his Land the most colorful place that one could find. With that dream in his heart he began his journey back home.

He started using his imagination to find a way to go up into the sky and reach the Black and White rainbow.

He thought… and he thought….to the point that he found a solution:

"That's it! I'm going to follow the rainbow all the way till I find its end. Then when I find the end of the rainbow, I'll jump on to it!"

Leonardo waited for the rain to come…

Then one day it rained and the rainbow appeared across the sky. It was beautiful! But it had only the same two colors: Black and White.

He then started his search to find the end of the rainbow.

He walked, and walked, and walked ... but he never found the rainbow's end.

So he thought again, and said to himself:

"I think that with a ladder I could get up on to the rainbow."

Leonardo started searching for the tallest ladder that ever existed! But after searching for days, and searching everywhere, he got tired.

Sadly he could not find a ladder that could take him high enough into the sky.

He was sad for a moment, since he thought he would never be able to pursue his dream to color the Black and White rainbow.

But he was not one to give up!

"No, I'm not going to give up now; I must find a way to get to the rainbow." At that moment, Leonardo looked up to the sky and said:

"I know some day I'll get there, and I'll turn the Land of Black and White into a colorful and happy Land."

Suddenly, as if by magic, a flock of beautiful white doves appeared out of nowhere crossing the sky. With excitement Leonardo shouted:

"Wow, how could I not have thought of that before!? I can get many doves together, tie them up with a string, and they will take me up in the air, all the way up to the rainbow.

So he scattered lots of corn grains on the ground, and it didn't take long before the doves came to eat the corn.

Leonardo let them eat as much as they wanted. What a great meal!

As the doves got stronger he put them together with the string and they flew away, taking with them the dreamful boy holding on to the end of the string.

Flying high, and getting higher every minute.

They flew over the highest mountains, and around the sun and the moon.

After flying over the whole world, Leonardo finally got to the end of his journey. His dream was now reality.

He was on the Black and White rainbow!

He set the doves free, and was so grateful for their help!

They flew away, happy for having been able to help Leonardo pursue his dream.

From up there he looked down at the Land of Black and White, and he could even see the far away Land of Colors.

Leonardo was ready to start painting the Black and White rainbow!

Tragically, as he turned to use the colors, he realized that he had forgotten to bring them. "I left behind all the colors!" He screamed.

At that very instant, Leonardo felt the same way he felt when he woke up and his heart was speaking of colors.

Only this time, his heart started radiating the most incredible colors, as if from the most beautiful flowers, from the most spectacular gardens that ever existed!

The colors wouldn't stop flowing, and the once Black and White rainbow was now the most colorful one in the entire universe!

Leonardo to this day, lives in the Land of Thousands of Colors.

About The Author

Dr. Fabiano Rabelo DeMoraes has written three children's books, and also poems and poetry. He started writing at the early age of 12.

He has been awarded best poem in various categories, supporting his passion to write and create stories.

He dedicated himself to children after graduating as an Oral Surgeon, and specializing in Pediatrics and Endodontics.

The experience with children and their dreams had always inspired him to write and tell stories, creating fantasy worlds that children can relate to.

Lightning Source UK Ltd.
Milton Keynes UK
UKHW051249281119
354389UK00005B/83/P